Powder

by
Ian MacDonald

Illustrated by Vince Reid

First Published
March 09 in Great Britain by

PUBLISHING

© Ian MacDonald 2009

ISBN-10: 1-905637-65-9
ISBN-13: 978-1-905637-65-2

Educational Printing Services Limited
Albion Mill, Water Street, Great Harwood, Blackburn BB6 7QR
Telephone: (01254) 882080   Fax: (01254) 882010
E-mail: enquiries@eprint.co.uk   Website: www.eprint.co.uk

Contents

A Puff of Smoke

"Fire away!"

Jack pressed his thumb down hard on the computer game pad in his hand.

On the tiny screen spaceships and aliens zigzagged across a blank sky. Every time Jack's finger hit the button another alien exploded in a puff of green smoke.

"I can see the sea!" shouted Sarah Martin from somewhere at the back of the coach.

"Wow! Look at all the boats!"

"Miss, what are all them poles sticking up?"

"Masts, Nathan, they're called masts," said Mrs Hardy, "and they're not boats, either. They're called ships."

All the children crowded at the window to see.

"Jack, you haven't looked up from that thing the whole journey!" frowned the teacher. "Don't you want to see what's going on outside...in the real world!"

Jack made no reply. Another alien became a puff of smoke.

"Jack Hawkins, I'm talking to you!"

The teacher leaned over and snatched the game out of the schoolboy's hand. Picking up the rucksack at his feet, she stuffed the plastic toy deep inside.

Jack slouched back in his seat and turned his face away.

"I don't know why you bothered coming on this trip," sighed the teacher.

* * * * *

"Welcome aboard Nelson's flagship, the HMS *Victory*."

A man in sailor's uniform stood in front of the children.

"We are going to begin our tour on the top deck. Please follow me. Mind the step as we go up."

Abby Hopkins pushed forward to walk beside the tall sailor, while others crowded close to hear what he was saying. Pages turned in notebooks as they climbed some stairs and stepped out into the wind.

Out on the top deck tall masts, like great trees, towered above them and rope ladders seemed to climb into the clouds.

"That's called the rigging," said the guide, seeing the children squinting up at the tops of the masts. "Imagine having to climb up there when the wind is blowing and the ship is pitching in rough seas."

They came to a place where there was a polished brass plate on the deck. "The *Victory* was Nelson's flagship during the Battle of Trafalgar. The Battle was fought on 21 October, 1805. This plate marks the spot where Nelson fell, hit by a French sniper's bullet."

Jack stood at the back, not listening. Soon they would return to the coach and go to the place where they would be staying for the week. Then he could shut the door and get back to his computer game.

Now the sailor led them down some stairs and they came to another floor on the ship. Next to where they stood was a large, black cannon. It was mounted on a kind of wooden carriage with wheels. All along the side identical cannons were lined up, facing out of square holes, like windows in the side of the ship.

"This is the upper gun deck where everything happened in times of battle. Every gun had its own gun crew. Every man in the gun crew had a job to do. There was even a boy about your age, I guess – he was called the powder monkey – it was his job to fetch the powder to fire the guns."

Now Lucy Pemberton was asking a question. No one was looking. Jack knelt down and rested his rucksack on the floor. There were his initials on it.

J.H.

His mum had put them there. He was always losing his bag.

He reached inside and fumbled around until his fingers found the touch of smooth plastic. He drew his game out carefully, and flicked the 'on' switch. The screen lit up and the first alien appeared, moving sideways across the screen, daring Jack to blast him out of the sky.

The guide was answering Lucy's question, but Jack did not hear. He had not listened to a word the whole afternoon. He did not hear the warning as the group moved off again. He did not see the children stooping under the low beam.

"Mind your heads, please!"

Whack!

Jack's head thundered...

...and everything went black.

Fantastic Facts: HMS Victory

HMS *Victory* was Nelson's flagship at the Battle of Trafalgar.

➤ The *Victory* was launched at Chatham Dockyard in 1765. Built almost entirely of wood, it took about 6,000 trees to make.

➤ The *Victory* is nearly 70 metres long.

➤ It has three masts called the foremast, the main mast and the mizzen mast. The top of the main mast is more than 60 metres above the waterline.

➤ When ready for battle there were 820 men on board. A fully-armed fighting ship, the *Victory* carried 100 guns.

Salty Sayings: Has anyone ever told you that you are *swinging the lead?* They mean you are trying to get away with something. In Nelson's day a lead rod was swung over the side of the ship to measure the depth of the sea bed – *swinging the lead*!

Powder Monkey

"Powder monkey!"

Jack looked up.

There was smoke everywhere. People were shouting. The air seemed to burn, and the hot smell of sweat filled his throat and lungs.

Then, slowly, as the smoke began to

clear, several figures appeared out of the black fog.

There were four or five of them, all men, some stripped to the waist, others in striped shirts and baggy white trousers. They were crowded around the cannon, their backs turned to Jack. They called out to each other as they strained at their work. Some of them carried large poles with a cloth or a metal hook at the end. Another man held a large iron ball in his hands.

At that moment, one of the men turned and looked at Jack.

"Powder monkey!" he roared. "Look lively, there! Fetch another bag o' powder – and quick about it."

Jack staggered to his feet. He looked

behind him, to see who the man was talking to. But there was no one else there.

"What's the matter, boy? Don't you understand the King's English? Stir yourself or I'll box your ears for you."

Jack rubbed his eyes and glanced down.

It was like looking down at someone else's body. Where there should have been trainers, jeans and a sweatshirt, he saw bare feet, a pair of baggy white trousers and a striped shirt.

Suddenly, there was a deafening explosion, and more smoke filled the air. From out of the black cloud came a great dark shape. Almost too late, Jack saw the back end of the cannon coming towards him. He threw himself sideways as the huge wheels came to a halt, inches from where he had just been standing.

Jack felt a hand tug at his shirt and pull him to his feet.

"Follow me," said a voice.

Jack looked to his left. There was a boy about his own age, dressed in much the same way. The boy set off, dodging between pillars, across to the other side of the ship. Another gun sounded behind them, shaking the deck beneath their bare feet.

"This way," said the boy as they came upon a line of sailors passing along a wooden box that looked a bit like a chimney pot.

Then they came to an open hatch with stairs that led down to the next deck. And, as the boys arrived, another box was thrown up from below. A man at the top caught it and held it out to Jack.

Jack just stood there, not knowing what to do. Someone else pushed past and grabbed the box instead. Then another one appeared and this time Jack took it in his arms. Now he could see it was made of wood and had a rope handle at one end. Following the boy, Jack set off back the way they had come.

They arrived back to another cloud of
black smoke. Jack watched as the boy bent
down and took out two small white sacks
from the chimney-pot box. There was
another box on the deck, this time with
straight sides. The boy put the two bags
inside this one.

"Powder monkey!" came a shout from
nearby.

Jack got the idea. He took out a white sack. It was about twice the size of a bag of flour.

"Come on, boy, look lively with it!"

Jack handed the bag to the man who had called out. He watched as it was passed along to the front of the cannon. There it disappeared into the end. A third man pushed a long pole into the cannon in a lightning fast movement, followed by a black metal ball. Then he stepped back. From somewhere at Jack's elbow someone else pulled on a string. There was a deafening sound like thunder, and then a puff of black smoke.

The boys made the trip three times to collect more gunpowder.

"Who are we fighting?" shouted Jack, trying to make himself heard against the roar of the cannons.

"Fighting?" laughed the boy, "Lord save us! This is only gun practice."

Fantastic Facts: The Guns

Cannons on board ship were called guns. HMS *Victory* carried a hundred guns on its three gun decks.

➢ A gun crew could clean a gun barrel, reload and fire in just 90 seconds. This was much quicker than the French and Spanish could manage.

➢ The gun crew used special tools on long poles to clean and load the gun. One of these was called the *worm*. It was used to hook out any bits and pieces left from firing the previous round.

➢ Small bags of powder were passed up from the magazine in *pass boxes*, which were cylinder shaped. They were then put in square-sided *salt boxes* near the guns ready for use.

➤ The guns usually fired cannonballs but sometimes *chain shot*, with chains and weights, would be used to bring down a ship's rigging. *Grape shot* (like a bunch of grapes) sent a cluster of smaller cannonballs exploding across the deck.

bar shot

chain shot

Salty Sayings: Ever heard someone say, "It's *brass monkeys* out there!" meaning it's bitterly cold? A brass monkey was where you stacked the cannon balls. So... "*it's cold enough to freeze the cannonballs on a brass monkey.*"

Ship's Biscuits

"Cease firing!"

A loud voice echoed down the deck as a last explosion sounded at the far end of the ship. All along the deck men stood panting, sweat glistening on their tired bodies.

Jack stood still, watching the smoke drift by. He was aware of someone standing at his shoulder. It was the boy who had come to his rescue a moment ago.

"My name's Will. Who are you?" asked the boy.

"Jack. Jack Hawkins."

"You're a rum 'un, and no mistake. I haven't seen you on this deck before."

"I came from...up there." Jack pointed somewhere above his head.

"What's a powder monkey doing up there? There are no guns on the top deck, save the carronades."

Jack looked about him, searching for some familiar sight. Perhaps this was one of those history plays that were put on to show schoolchildren what it was like in the old days. But everything here seemed horribly real.

Jack looked over Will's shoulder. A table had appeared, as if from nowhere, and was now hung from ropes between two of the cannons. Wooden plates and cups were already laid out.

"This way, boy," said one of the sailors. "I need some food to line my belly."

Jack looked across at Will, who simply nodded.

Jack followed the sailor down some stairs and found himself on another deck. It was much like the one they had just left. But here there were soldiers in red uniforms, some polishing long rifles. Then more stairs, and another gun deck. Jack began to wonder just how many more decks there could be.

Then they came to a counter where a sailor filled their bowls from two or three different barrels. He also gave them some red meat and a round, hard-looking bread.

Returning with a bowl in each hand, Jack stopped in his tracks. Blocking his way was a large pig. He rubbed his eyes. The pig was still there.

"Come here, you scurvy porker." Three sailors were hurrying towards the pig from the other direction. The pig looked back at the men, and then he looked at the small boy in his path. The men began to run, and so did the pig – straight at Jack.

Juggling the bowls in his hands, Jack tried to get out of the way. He hopped to the left, then changed his mind and stepped back. Too late – the pig hit him somewhere between his knees. Oats and dried peas flew everywhere. The pig squealed loudly and Jack fell forward. He felt the pig's snout come up underneath him. Jack now found himself carried along, staring into the wrong end of a pig.

"Hey, come back with our dinner!" roared the sailors.

The pig ran to the end of the gangway, and swerved left.

Jack tumbled to the deck.

By the time he had cleared up the mess, the men at his table had nearly finished their meal. Jack sat down at last and began to eat. His bowl contained a kind of stew with meat, peas and oats mixed in.

He watched as the men tapped the round bread on the table before they ate it. Jack picked up his bread and took a bite. It was hard, more like a biscuit. It felt cold and his tongue tickled. He looked at what was left in his hand. Something was wiggling in his bread.

He took a closer look, and spat his mouthful onto the floor.

Maggots.

Fantastic Facts: Food

If you thought school dinners were bad, you should try the food on board ship!

➢ There were no fridges then. To keep your meat fresh it was best to have it walking round on four legs!

➢ Beef or pork was also packed in salt to stop it from going bad. It took hours of soaking in water to get rid of the salty taste.

➢ *Ship's biscuits* were often crawling with maggots, so the crew often took them back to their beds...to eat in the dark!

➢ Barrels of drinking water soon went stale. Sailors drank beer, wine or *rum*. Rum was often mixed with lime juice to prevent a disease called *scurvy*.

Salty Sayings: Someone who is staggering about, like a boxer who has taken too many punches, is said to be *groggy*. This probably comes from sailors who drank too much *grog*, the sailor's name for watered-down rum.

Portsmouth Harbour

Jack awoke early.

He lay in the darkness for a moment, trying to picture the walls of his bedroom at home. But the swaying of the ship brought back the memory of the day just gone. He turned over, threatening to tip himself out of his bed. Last night, Will had shown him how to fasten his hammock, a length of canvas tied to hooks in the beams. It was difficult to climb into. He had fallen out twice before he had managed to settle down and pull his blanket up to his chin.

It was just as hard to climb out, but Jack managed to steady himself enough to clamber out onto the wooden deck. Tip-toeing past the swinging hammocks of the sleeping gunners, he made his way up on to the top deck. He looked out over the dark water.

The first glimpse of daylight showed, casting a pink glow over the sea. In the distance Jack could see land. He could just make out the masts of ships showing against the rooftops of grey buildings. A hill, like a great black whale, loomed high over the landscape, a few lights winking at the windows of houses.

"You're up with the lark!" Will came and leaned over the rail at Jack's side.

"Where are we?" asked Jack.

"Portsmouth Harbour, of course," said Will.

"Portsmouth, but...I don't recognise anything."

"We're going ashore...to look for my father."

"What do you mean?" asked Jack, looking puzzled.

"When I was five years old my father went to buy spices from the trade ships. It was meant to be a treat for Mother...but he never came back. I never found out what happened to him."

Jack did not know what to say.

"Come on, the bosun is stirring the men from their hammocks," said Will, wiping his eyes with the back of his hand.

Breakfast was a bowl of grey-looking porridge, which the sailors called burgoo. And more ship's biscuits. This time Jack went without. He wondered how long it would be before he became so hungry that he would have to eat them again.

After breakfast the two boys made
their way on deck and watched as their ship
dropped anchor. They were some way out
from the dockside but Jack could see
people, like scurrying ants, busy wheeling
trolleys or lifting barrels. A few men were
unloading sacks from a cart that was pulled
by a great carthorse. The supplies were put
into small boats and rowed out to be loaded
aboard the *Victory*.

Suddenly, there was a great cheer
from the harbour walls. The boys leaned
over the rail to see what was happening.
Will looked about him and spotted an
officer's telescope lying nearby. He dashed
over and picked it up, handing it to Jack.

Through the round window of the
telescope, Jack saw a man step from a
carriage. His long, grey hair blew in the

breeze and he carried a black hat. He wore
a short blue coat decorated with gold.

Jack wondered why the man had one
of his sleeves pinned to the outside of his
jacket. Then he realised: the sleeve was
empty; the man had only one arm. Jack
wondered what use such a man would be on a
fighting ship.

"Hurray, for the Admiral," called Will,
and aboard the ship and all along the
harbour side, men raised their hats in
salute. Everyone stopped what they were
doing to cheer.

Jack looked puzzled.

"There's a hero, if ever there was one!" said Will. "Admiral Lord Nelson, God bless him!"

Fantastic Facts: Lord Nelson

Admiral Horatio Nelson led the British fleet to victory over the French and Spanish at the Battle of Trafalgar.

- ➤ He joined the navy at the age of 12. He lost an eye and his right arm in an earlier sea battle.

- ➤ Although he had a wife, Nelson also had a girlfriend called Lady Emma Hamilton. Nelson wrote her many passionate love letters while he was away at sea.

- ➤ At the height of the Battle of Trafalgar, Nelson was shot by a French marksman firing from the rigging of the *Redoubtable*. He was taken down to the orlop - the lowest deck - where he died three hours later.

➢ Usually, sailors who died in battle were thrown overboard, but Nelson wanted to be buried in an English churchyard. His body was brought back in a barrel of brandy...to stop his body from rotting! The story goes that the sailors had drunk the barrel dry by the time they got back to Portsmouth...but this is probably not true!

Salty Sayings: To *turn a blind eye* means to overlook something on purpose. It was Nelson who put a telescope to his blind eye to ignore a signal to retreat. Of course, he went on to win the battle anyway!

Going Ashore

"Now's our chance," said Will.

Jack looked down at the rowing boat bobbing about on the water below. There were people everywhere. Officers watched as the supplies came on board. Several of the red-coated marines stood guard with their rifles at the ready.

"While everyone's watching the

Admiral come aboard," continued Will, "we can slip down the gangplank."

He set off, Jack close behind. Coming to the first open hatchway, Will looked around and found what he was looking for. Several empty barrels waiting to be taken ashore. He lifted one onto his shoulder and nodded to Jack to do the same. They both clambered into the rowing boat.

The boat rocked as the men pulled on the oars.

Will pulled out a crumpled piece of paper from inside his jacket. He handed it to Jack.

Even though it was only a faded pencil sketch, it was possible to see that it was a picture of a man with a bushy beard and bright, twinkling eyes.

"He was the village blacksmith," said Will. "He made horseshoes and fitted them on the horses. Sometimes I worked the bellows, blowing air into the fire to make it hot."

"What happened...after your dad left?"

"My mother had no money to keep us both, and I had to go to an orphanage. Then I was sent away to join the navy."

There was a bump as the rowing boat reached the dockside.

"Come on, then," said Will. They waited for two others to climb some stone steps and then the boys followed. At the top they put down their barrels, and slipped away.

Jack and Will set off, heading away from the harbour into the busy town. They stopped at shops and at market stalls showing the picture. But everywhere they went, they met the same answer. "No, never seen him."

Others simply waved the boys away without as much as a glance.

Once, on the outskirts of the old city, they came upon a blacksmith's shop. Inside, a man was bent over fixing a shoe on a big carthorse's hoof. Will stepped inside and called out. The blacksmith stopped and looked up. When he saw the two boys he shouted angrily, and Jack and Will hurried away, disappointed.

Further on, Will pulled Jack into a shop doorway as two men in uniform were leading another man, his hands chained together.

"Press gang," said Will.

"What's that?"

"When the drink wears off he'll find himself aboard some ship bound for Spain."

"What? Even if he doesn't want to go?"

"The navy needs extra fighting men in wartime," explained Will.

Then, as they stepped out of the doorway, two boys charged into them, knocking them to the ground.

"There they are," shouted a voice. Pointing at them from the end of the narrow roadway were several men. One of them carried a large stick. Another had a fierce-looking dog, already straining at his lead.

"Run!" shouted Will, dragging Jack into a dark alleyway.

"But..." spluttered Jack.

"Those boys have probably stolen someone's watch, and they think it's us!"

The two boys ran as fast as they could along dark alleyways and narrow passages, coming at last to the harbour again. They

could still hear the shouts of the men
behind them and the barking of the dog.
Racing across the cobblestones they came to
the steps which led down to the water.
They were in luck. A boat was waiting. A
sailor was putting the last sack into place.
The boys clambered into the boat and
ducked down behind the sacks.

"Keep down," hissed Will. They could hear the voices of the men. The dog began to bark. Jack and Will crouched low, holding their breath. The dog's barking became louder, but his owner spoke sharply to it and the dog gave a yelp. The dog began to whine and then the voices died away.

On the way back to the ship, Jack thought again about the man who was taken by the press gang. He wondered whether this was what might have happened to Will's dad. He was about to say something when he caught his friend's sad expression. And he said nothing.

Fantastic Facts: Punishment

Discipline at sea was very harsh. Here are
some of the punishments that were handed
out:

➢ The *bosun's starter*: A whack with a
   thick piece of rope across your
   shoulders was used to make the sailors
   work faster.

➢ Cat-o'-nine-tails: for serious offences
   you could face a flogging by the 'cat'.
   This was a piece of rope with nine 'tails'
   each knotted at the end. Floggings
   were always carried out with the crew
   assembled on deck, as a warning to
   everyone.

➢ Leg irons: A sailor awaiting punishment might have his legs fastened in iron hoops fixed to a metal bar on deck. There he would be fed only bread and water.

➢ Hanging: For very serious offences such as mutiny (disobeying orders) an offender could be hung from the *yard arm*.

Salty Sayings: When we say *rubbing salt into the wound* we mean making things worse. But, after a flogging, the ship's surgeon rubbed salt into wounds to stop them from going bad. "Ouch!"

Man the Rigging

"One, two, three, four, five..."

Jack sat in his hammock counting the marks on a piece of wood.

He had decided to keep a calendar by cutting notches with his eating knife. He had first stood on the *Victory* at the start of September. He was just a schoolboy then. It was now the middle of October.

Portsmouth Harbour was a long way behind them; they were now nearing the coast of Spain.

Jack had an idea. Jumping down, he went over to the place where he worked with the gun crew. No one was watching. Reaching up, he took down the fire bucket and carved his initials on the back.

J.H.

It was as if he was trying to prove that, at least for the moment, this was where he belonged.

"All hands on deck, there's a storm blowing!"

Jack put his things away and went up onto the top deck. There was plenty of activity. Several sailors were already climbing the rigging to take in the sails. The ship was starting to roll heavily in the high seas. Just then there was a yell. Jack looked up to see one of the men slip. His feet came away from the ropes. A heavy wave hit the side of the ship, and the masts tilted. The man tried hard to cling on, but the lower ropes were wet with spray. And then he fell. He hit the deck with a thud. Two men rushed over and the injured sailor rolled over and groaned. The men lifted him and began to carry him away, off to the sick-bay in the lower part of the ship.

"You there, boy," shouted a voice, "man the rigging."

Jack turned his head to see who the man was shouting at. But there was no one else. "But..."

"Don't answer me back, lad, or you'll taste the bosun's starter."

The sailor held a thick piece of rope in his hand. Jack had seen this used before on anyone who was not working fast enough. He did not want to feel the rope across his shoulders.

Jack ran to the side. He leaned over and looked at the grey water. Waves rose and fell, sending spray high into the air.

"What are you waiting for, boy?" roared the bosun's mate. Jack grabbed hold of the nearest rope. He pulled himself up until he was standing on the rail. The wood was wet and he had to hold tight to the rigging to stop himself from slipping. Then, taking a deep breath, Jack swung his body up onto the ropes, and began to climb.

Jack glanced down at the angry waves below. At that moment the whole ship tipped sideways. Jack pressed his body into the ropes to keep himself from letting go. He had heard stories of sailors who had fallen into the sea. He knew they could never turn the ship in time to rescue anybody.

"Quick about yourself, boy!" came a voice from above.

He began climbing again, trying not to look down. Hand by hand...step by step... climbing ever upwards. It seemed like climbing into the sky. But then Jack reached the topsail which flapped like an angry ghost, threatening to knock him from his perch. Then, further up and he was level with the great wooden beam which held the sail.

The other sailors were waiting. Jack remembered when he had seen the men on the yard arm before. It seemed like they were standing on air. But he could see now that their feet balanced on thin ropes under the yard arm.

That was what he was going to have to do.

Fantastic Facts: Know the Ropes

There are ropes for almost everything on board ship: ropes to raise the sails; ropes to hang your hammock from; even ropes to climb to the top of the mast.

➢ A ship's speed is measured in knots. A piece of wood was let over the side on a length of rope with knots in it. The number of knots which ran out was counted to find the speed. The *Victory's* top speed was 11 knots.

➢ The rigging was the name given to the rope ladders which rose to the mast tops. If you lay out the *Victory's* rigging in a single long rope, it would stretch an amazing 26 miles (42 km).

➢ Rope netting runs along the ship's side where sailors stowed their hammocks. This gave extra protection against musket shot during a battle. A hole in your hammock was better than a hole in the head!

➤ If you died while at sea you would be sewn into your hammock before being dropped into the sea. The last stitch went through your nose...to check you weren't just taking a nap!

Salty Sayings: The huge anchor rope was pulled in using smaller ropes called *nippers*. After a while the name *nipper* was given to the small boys who pulled these ropes. That's why small children are called *nippers* today!

"One Hand, Boy!"

The nearest sailor beckoned Jack out
along the yard arm. Jack felt the sweat cold
on his forehead. He put out his foot but it
simply waved in the air. He had to look down
to place his foot on the rope.

"Hurry up, boy!" shouted a rough voice.
"Let's get this sail trimmed. This storm
wants to blow us all to kingdom come."

Jack tried again and this time he found a foothold. Carefully, he edged his other foot off the rigging and shuffled his way out onto the yard arm. He clung on, wrapping both arms tightly around the wooden beam.

The ship gave another lurch sideways.

"One hand, boy," shouted one of the men.

And then his throat went dry when he realised what the sailor meant. The others were only holding on with one hand. With the other they pulled on ropes to bring in the sail.

Jack clenched his teeth and let go with one hand. There were ropes everywhere. Watching the other sailors' every move, Jack pulled on the ropes until the sail came towards them. He could see now that, with fewer sails to catch the wind, the ship would steady itself in the storm.

It seemed to take forever. Eventually, though, the sailors signalled to each other to tie off the ropes and clamber back down.

Gratefully, Jack made his way back across the yard arm to the rigging. But, just as he started to climb down, another wave caught the side of the ship and the mast lurched again. Jack felt his foot slip and one hand came free. He swung his arm, grabbing wildly at the air. He grasped at the nearest thing he could to stop himself from falling.

"Let go, you scurvy rat!" screamed a voice.

Jack had taken hold of a sailor's foot.
The man began shaking his leg, trying to
free himself. Jack felt his hand slipping...
slipping...then he let go. He closed his eyes,
waiting for the fall.

Immediately, he felt a strong hand
grab his wrist. He looked up into a bearded
face. In the next second he felt himself
swung around until he was back on the
rigging. Without stopping to thank his
rescuer, Jack scrambled down the ropes as
fast as he could go.

At the bottom he jumped down, landing in a heap on the deck. Before he could stand, someone grabbed him roughly by the collar. He turned to see the sailor whose foot he had grabbed earlier.

"You could have pitched me into the sea, you young rascal. I'll skin you alive, so help me!" the man screamed.

Jack saw the man raise his arm, but the blow never landed.

"I would not strike the boy if I were you," said a voice. Jack looked up from the deck.

There was Admiral Nelson, his grey hair blowing in the wind. He spoke sharply to the sailor. "I was a ship's boy once, and I am sure that you were too. I see you have come to no harm. Now, go below and attend to your duties."

The sailor bowed his head. "I beg your pardon, Admiral Nelson, sir. I meant no offence, your lordship."

Nelson nodded and the man hurried away.

Jack got to his feet, but already the admiral had stepped smartly away to the quarter deck, where several sailors were struggling with the ship's wheel.

"Are you alright?" said Will, rushing up to his friend.

"Yes, I think so," said Jack. "Thanks to..." He looked up. Standing there was a burly man with red hair and a bushy beard. "This was the man who..." Jack began, but his friend was not listening.

Will was gazing open-mouthed at the huge man with the twinkling eyes. "Dad?" he said.

England Expects

Jack was woken by the sound of two people talking in low voices.

A little morning light spilled in from the open gun ports. He took his stick calendar from under his pillow and counted the marks.

21st October.

Carefully turning over, Jack could just make out the large figure of a man standing beside Will's hammock. The sound of their voices drifted his way.

"Dad, why did you leave us?" Will asked.

"I never meant to go, son. It was the press gang, see. One minute I was in Portsmouth Town, buying a present for your mum...the next, I woke up with a thumping headache on a ship bound for Spain."

"But why you?"

"Well, take a look at me, Will. A big strong man like me is a good catch for the press gang. But, I swear, if we both get out of this alive today, God help us, we'll go back to your mum together."

Jack felt he should not listen to any more. He had been right about the press gang, though. He thought for a moment of his own family, and wondered if he would ever see them again. He wondered, too, what Will's father meant about "getting out of this alive".

Jack climbed out of his hammock and made his way up onto the weather deck. On every side the masts of the English fleet filled the sky, their red and white flags fluttering in the light breeze.

The upper decks were packed with men: the white-shirted sailors, the red coats of the marines and the blue jackets of the officers. And there, on the poop deck, was Admiral Nelson talking to the tall figure of Captain Hardy. Everyone was looking out into the distance where a faint grey line of ships could just be seen, their masts drawn like pencil lines on the pale sky.

"Who are they?" breathed Jack.

"That's the French and Spanish making ready for battle," said Will, appearing at Jack's shoulder.

"But, there's so many of them."

"Sound the beat to quarters," called an officer. The drummer sounded out the order.

"We'd better go," said Will, as the sailors started to go below.

"Just a minute longer," said Jack.

Then, looking up, Jack saw a line of flags, strung out across the mast head like washing on a line. A cheer came from the nearest ship, the *Téméraire* which now almost stood alongside the *Victory*.

"What do the flags mean?" said Jack.

The signalman, standing nearby, saw the two boys and read the message aloud to them.

ENGLAND EXPECTS THAT EVERY MAN
WILL DO HIS DUTY

And then the *Téméraire* drew back, and the *Victory* led the English line again.

"To your posts, you boys there," called one of the officers. And Jack and Will hurried away.

Below decks, everything was cleared for battle.

"Powder monkey!" shouted a voice.

Jack ran to the hatch as the pass boxes began to come. He had now become quite good at catching the round cases as they were passed along the line. As each one came he returned to fill up the wooden boxes, as he had done so many times before. But this was no gun drill. This time another ship would be firing back.

He looked down at the pile of cannon balls neatly stacked. He tried not to think of one of those flying through the air in his direction.

He watched as the crew loaded their first round, the strange tools on long poles each pushed into the hole at the end of the cannon: the metal hook cleaning out the barrel, then the powder charge, then the rammer to pack it home...and then the cannon ball. The gun set, the string wrapped tightly around the finger of the last man. All was ready.

And everything became quiet. It was almost like being in church. Men stood at their guns in silence. One or two leaned out of the gun ports to watch as they drew nearer to the enemy. Here and there, one or two strong men even knelt down by their gun carriages to pray.

Some stood chewing on bread and cheese. Jack realised it must be lunchtime, but he was too scared to eat. He felt the sweat break out on the back of his neck, and run cold down his back, soaking his shirt.

But still, he could not stop himself from looking out of a gun port.

"Where are our ships?" he gasped.

Enemy ships filled the skyline.

But Jack could see no English ships at all. He looked about him in a panic. But then he saw them, formed up in a long line behind the *Victory*. And further out, across the waves, was another line of British ships, also heading for the French and Spanish fleet.

Will came and pressed close to his friend to see. "We're going to break through the enemy lines," he whispered.

"But...we're facing their broadside," muttered Jack, "and we're going to get there first."

"We're a sitting target," said Will.

Fire and Blood

Jack wondered just what Admiral Nelson was planning. It seemed madness. Sailing head on at the side of the enemy ships – and their guns – was asking for trouble. The *Victory* at the front would take most of the damage, and would not be able to fire a shot until she had broken through the line.

He tried to imagine the admiral

standing on the quarter deck, his medals on show, a target for any French rifleman who might spot him from the rigging.

Just then a white puff of cloud appeared from the side of one of the ships, and the sound of a shot followed. Something skimmed the water in front of them. White water exploded in a cloud of spray.

"They're firing on us," said someone nearby.

"Stand at your posts. Hold fire until the order's given," called out one of the officers.

Jack left the gun port and stood by the powder boxes, ready.

All faces were turned towards the young officer. He looked no more than a boy himself, perhaps nineteen or twenty. Once the battle began it would be impossible to hear any orders anyway. But everyone stood, awaiting the first order to fire.

Jack could hear the low boom of the cannons, firing steadily now. There was a crash as something hit the water not far away. He remembered something Will had said, that the French were no good at aiming in a rolling sea. He hoped he was right.

Just then there was a loud, splintering sound above their heads.

"The mizzen mast..." shouted a voice nearby.

Then a crash as something thudded over their heads. The crew tensed in the half darkness.

Now the explosions from outside were deafening, like the sound of thunder. They were close in among the French now. Again the splintering of wood. There were shouts from further down the ship. Two men came past carrying a limp body.

"Gawd help us, how long are we going to wait," hissed Thomas Fariner, straining on the gun rope.

"You'll wait for the order!" shouted the officer.

And then a cry and the first guns sounded from the *Victory*'s gun ports. The whiff of gunpowder caught the air and explosions rippled down the deck, then down the gun deck below, until the whole ship seemed to heave and rise out of the water, with the battering of a hundred guns all firing together.

The air became black with smoke, shouts and screams echoed in the darkness; the deck shook as the cannons sprang backwards and the ropes strained to hold them. All the while Jack worked hard, fetching the pass boxes and handing on the powder bags.

"Powder monkey!" a voice shouted above the din.

Jack turned to take another bag from the powder box, but a deafening explosion sounded behind him. He turned. The wooden wall in front of him seemed to lift, and then sink. Then the air about him became suddenly hot, and he felt something pass by his left shoulder. There was a deafening crack, and Jack felt the deck beneath him shudder. He put out his hands to save himself, but there was nothing there.

* * * * *

"...and Nelson died, shot by a French marksman in the rigging of the *Redoubtable*. He was taken down to the orlop deck, where he died, but not before hearing that the Battle of Trafalgar had been won..."

Jack recognised the voice. He forced his eyes open. There was the old sailor and the schoolchildren gathered around him.

"Are you alright, Jack?" said Mrs Hardy. "You've had a nasty bump. I think we need to get you back to the coach."

Jack leaned forward to stand up. His head swam. Reaching out to steady himself, he knocked something from a hook above his head. The object clattered to the ground. It rolled over and then came to a standstill at his feet.

Jack bent down and picked it up. It was a fire bucket. On one side was painted the royal crest of King George in bright gold paint.

He turned it over in his hands.

And there, on the back, in letters so faint you could hardly see, someone had carved two letters:

J.H.

Fantastic Facts: Trafalgar

The Battle of Trafalgar is regarded as one of the greatest sea victories ever won. It meant that the French Emperor, Napoleon, would have to give up his plans to invade Britain.

➢ The Battle of Trafalgar was fought off Cape Trafalgar, near Cadiz, on the coast of Spain. It took place on 21st October, 1805.

➢ The British were outnumbered. They had twenty-seven fighting ships against the French and Spanish Fleet of thirty-three.

➢ Nelson's daring plan was to sail his ships in two lines head-on at the enemy's 'broadside'. The English ships broke through enemy lines, separating many of their ships from the main fleet.

➢ Using their much quicker firing rate they soon destroyed much of the enemy fleet. By the end of the battle only eleven of the enemy ships were still afloat.

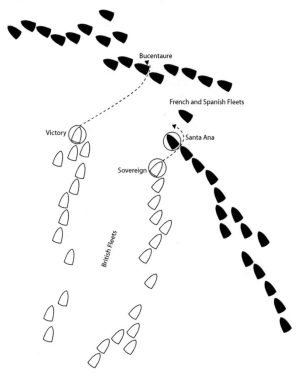

Bucentaure

French and Spanish Fleets

Victory

Santa Ana

Sovereign

British Fleets

Last Word: In Trafalgar Square, Nelson stands watch on his high column. This most famous London landmark helps to make sure we will not forget Nelson's great victory.

Word List

Here are some special words about ships to help you enjoy this book. You can read them before you begin the story, or look back if you find a word that you want to know.

bar shot	shaped like a weight lifter's bar bell, fired from the gun to break enemy masts.
burgoo	an oatmeal porridge served on board ship.
bosun	short for *Boatswain*. The officer in charge of sails and rigging.
bosun's mate	assistant to the bosun.
bosun's starter	a length of rope used to hit or 'start' a sailor who was not working fast enough (see page 47).
broadside	the side of the ship where

the guns are mounted ('firing a broadside').

carronade a powerful cannon mounted on the fo'csle firing 68 pounds of shot.

cases of wood cylinder-shaped boxes for carrying powder bags to the guns. They were also called *pass boxes* (see page 19).

chain shot two weights joined by a chain, fired to damage enemy rigging (see page 20).

foc'sle short for *fore-castle*. The rear part of old fighting ships looked like castles.

fleet a group of ships, e.g. the British Fleet.

frigate a smaller warship. Several frigates supported the fleet at the Battle of Trafalgar.

gangplank	a movable plank used to get on and off a ship or boat.
gun	cannons on board ship are called guns. Each gun had its own gun crew (see page 19).
grape shot	a canvas bag of smaller cannon balls which burst open, killing and wounding (see page 20).
hammock	a canvas 'bed' strung from hooks in wooden beams overhead.
magazine	the room where the gunpowder was kept.
orlop deck	the lowest of the decks.
pass boxes	boxes which carried the powder bags 'passed' in a line to the gun crew (see *cases of wood* and page 19).
powder monkey	a sailor who passed powder to the gun crew; often boys as young as 11 or 12.

port hole   a window in a ship, sometimes without glass. Guns poked out of open *gun ports*.

press gang   a group of men employed to force other men into the army or navy.

rammer   a hard pad on a long pole to ram the powder and shot into the gun barrel.

rum   an alcoholic drink. Sailors were issued a 'tot' of rum daily (see page 28).

salt boxes   a small, square-shaped box near the gun for keeping powder bags ready for use (see page 19).

scurvy   a disease caused by lack of vitamins in a sailor's diet (see page 28).

ship's biscuits   a round, flat bread, part of a sailor's diet (see page 28).

sponge   a wet, woollen pad on a long pole to dampen down sparks after firing the gun.

trim the sails   to take in the sails, for example in high winds.

worm(er)   a metal hook on a long pole to clean out bits and pieces after firing the gun (see page 19).

yard arm   the cross bars on the masts which hold the sails (see page 48).

Deadline *(Adventure)*
Sandra Glover   ISBN 978 1 904904 30 4

A Marrow Escape *(Adventure)*
Stephanie Baudet   ISBN 1 900818 82 5

The One That Got Away *(Humorous)*
Stephanie Baudet   ISBN 1 900818 87 6

The Haunted Windmill *(Mystery)*
Margaret Nash   ISBN 978 1 904904 22 9

Friday the Thirteenth *(Humorous)*
David Webb   ISBN 978 1 905637 37 9

Trevor's Trousers *(Humorous)*
David Webb   ISBN 978 1 904904 19

The Library Ghost *(Mystery)*
David Webb   ISBN 978 1 904374 66

Dinosaur Day *(Adventure)*
David Webb   ISBN 978 1 904374 67 1

Laura's Game *(Football)*
David Webb   ISBN 1 900818 61 2

Grandma's Teeth *(Humorous)*
David Webb   ISBN 978 1 905637 20 1

The Bears Bite Back *(Humorous)*
Derek Keilty   ISBN 978 1 905637 36 2

The Crash *(Mystery)*
Sandra Glover   ISBN 978 1 905637 29 4

The Owlers *(Adventure)*
Stephanie Baudet   ISBN 978 1 904904 87 8

Order online @ **www.eprint.co.uk**

Also available from:

PUBLISHING

The Mum Manager   *(Football)*
Suzi Cresswell   ISBN 978 1 905637 45 4

Sam's Spitfire Summer *(World War II Adventure)*
Ian MacDonald   ISBN 978 1 905637 43 0
www.authorinschools.co.uk

The Magician's Bag *(Adventure)*
Ian MacDonald   ISBN 978 1 905637 60 7

Skateboard Gran   *(Humorous)*
Ian MacDonald   ISBN 978 1 905637 30 0

Alien Teeth   *(Humorous Science Fiction)*
Ian MacDonald   ISBN 978 1 905637 32 2

Eyeball Soup   *(Science Fiction)*
Ian MacDonald   ISBN 978 1 904904 59 5

Chip McGraw   *(Cowboy Mystery)*
Ian MacDonald   ISBN 978 1 905637 08 9

Close Call   *(Mystery - Interest age 12+)*
Sandra Glover   ISBN 978 1 905 637 07 2

Beastly Things in the Barn *(Humorous)*
Sandra Glover   ISBN 978 1 904904 96 0
www.sandraglover.co.uk

Cracking Up   *(Humorous)*
Sandra Glover   ISBN 978 1 904904 86 1